THE TALE OF DOUBLE SIX

TAHIR SHAH

MISBAH BUKHARI

THE TALE OF DOUBLE SIX

TAHIR SHAH

MISBAH BUKHARI

MMXXIII

Secretum Mundi Publishing Ltd
124 City Road
London
EC1V 2NX
United Kingdom

www.secretum-mundi.com
info@secretum-mundi.com

First published by Secretum Mundi Publishing Ltd, 2023

THE TALE OF DOUBLE SIX

Artwork drawn by Misbah Bukhari

A CIP catalogue record for this title is available from the British Library.

ISBN 978-1-914960-98-7

VERSION 01022023

Visit the author's website:
Tahirshah.com

Once upon a time, when the clouds were pinker than pink and the great mountains were little higher than molehills, there lived a young woman named Farzana.

The daughter of a forester, she had grown up in a glade deep in the heart of the Forest of Eternal Solitude. Since childhood, she had wished to glimpse the world beyond the labyrinth of trees.

'Tomorrow I'm going to leave the forest and find the city,' she said to her parents one evening. 'To seek my fortune, and make you prouder than proud.'

Farzana's father regarded his
beloved daughter, the apple of his eye.
'Life is not a cage,' he said. 'And so, if you wish
to go to the city and seek your fortune, your
mother and I give our blessings.'

Next morning, before the dawn chorus had stirred the forest from its sleep, Farzana stood at the edge of the glade with a simple knapsack of provisions slung over her shoulder.

Hugging her daughter tight, her mother said: 'Always remember that you're the sun and the moon to us, and the stars in the heavens, too.' 'And always remember,' her father added, 'we will be waiting for you here at your home.'

Kissing her parents once, and then again,
Farzana set off through the forest
in search of her fortune.

Using the sun to guide her, she headed in the direction that she believed the great city lay.

Having grown up with the trees around her, her small feet moved nimbly. All she could think of were the thrills of the city that awaited her in a realm of frivolity and joy.

All day she walked, her mind imagining what her fortune might be like once she had broken free from the Forest of Eternal Solitude.

As the sun's light dimmed to dusk, Farzana stopped for the night. She ate the little meal she had brought with her, and listened to the owls hooting up in the high branches of the trees.

Then, making a pile of dry leaves, she lay down. She was about to fall fast asleep when she heard a rustling sound a stone's throw away.

At first, she assumed it was a creature
burrowing into the dry leaves for the night.
But, turning in the direction of the noise,
she realized it was a mongoose caught in
a poacher's trap.

Farzana got up off her makeshift bed, hurried over to the creature, and with great care managed to free it. To her surprise, the mongoose didn't dart away into the night. Rather, rearing up on its hind legs, it addressed the girl in her own tongue:

'You may have imagined that you were helping an innocent animal gain its freedom,' the mongoose said in a polite voice, 'but in actual fact, I am a jinn. The cruel device from which you freed me was no ordinary trap, but designed to ensnare a harmless jinn such as myself.'

Taken aback at encountering a creature from the supernatural realm, Farzana wished the jinn well, and made her way back to the pile of dry leaves that were about to serve as her bed.

As she reached the leaves, they transformed into a lovely mahogany bedstead, replete with crisp linen sheets and a thick woollen blanket.

As she wondered what was going on,
Farzana heard the voice of the
mongoose in the distance:
'A small act of kindness to
repay a far greater one…'

Giving thanks, Farzana climbed into the bed, and instantly fell asleep.

Next morning, she awoke from a dream – a dream featuring a trapped mongoose that was a jinn, and a fabulous mahogany bedstead. Wiping the sleep from her eyes, she grasped that the dream hadn't been a dream at all, and that the mongoose was curled up at the foot of the bed.

'Good morning,' the creature said. 'I hope you don't mind, but I curled up here so as to keep watch over you. After all, the forest is never quite as safe as one would wish it to be.'

Farzana was going to say something
when the jinn broke in:
'If you would permit me,' he said, 'I would
like to prepare a little breakfast for you.'
'Oh, well, er, thank you.'

Instantly, a tray was resting on the bedstead, its surface adorned with the most delicious foods imaginable.

Helping herself to the meal,
Farzana suddenly paused.
'How did you know that these are
my very favourite dishes?' she asked.

The mongoose blushed.

‘I took the liberty of having a quick
peek in your head,’ he said.
Now it was the daughter of the
forester who blushed.
‘Did you see any of my secrets?’

The mongoose swallowed.

'I shall never tell,' he answered. 'You saved me from a terrible fate, and so I am here to help you.'

Farzana sighed disapprovingly.
'Other than the foods I like most, what else did you find out while you were digging around in my thoughts?'

The jinn touched a paw to his chin.

‘That you are on your way to the city to make your fortune.’

‘That’s right.’

‘I can let you into a little secret,’
the mongoose said.

‘A secret?’

‘Yes. It’s that, as a jinn, I can see every chain of possible events being played out. And, as such, I know how best you can find your fortune.’

'By going to the city that lies beyond the Forest of Eternal Solitude?'

'No.'

'What do you mean, "No"?'

The mongoose cleared his throat.
'I mean that, by seeking your fortune in the city that lies beyond the forest, you won't have the fortune you desire.'
'Why not?'

‘Because,’ answered the jinn,
‘your destiny doesn’t lie there.’

Farzana stared down at the pattern on the blanket, her gaze rising to the mongoose's miniature face. 'If my destiny does not await me in the city beyond this forest, then where is it?'

Again, the mongoose
touched a paw to his chin

‘Destiny is a tricky thing,’ he said. ‘It’s not so simple as going to one place, and hoping that everything will take shape there just as you need it to.’

‘So, what ought I to do?’

The jinn extended a claw and
scratched the top of his head.

'Since you helped me, I'd like to help you in return,' he replied.

'How?' Farzana asked.

'When searching for one's destiny,' he said,
'it helps if you can see the invisible path
of your life.'
'How can I hope to see it if it's invisible?'

The mongoose let out a cackle.

'Well, as a human you have no hope of ever glimpsing the path,' he said. 'But as a jinn, I can see it. And I can transport you to the places and situations that will provide for you the most perfect form of fortune.'

Since earliest childhood, Farzana had heard fearful things about jinns and their nefarious ways. Everyone knew that jinns liked nothing more than deceiving humans.

'How can I be certain you won't trick me?' she asked point blank.

The mongoose thought for a moment.

Sitting up straight-backed, he replied:
'Because I have no reason to do so, and I have every reason to return the favour.'
'Very well,' Farzana said, 'take me to where the very best version of my destiny lies.'

‘Close your eyes,’ said the jinn.
‘Are you ready?’

The daughter of the forester
swallowed anxiously.
'Yes, I suppose I am.'

A clap of thunder.
The aroma of burnt sulphur.
A wind as ferocious as any that
has ever come or gone.

The mongoose cleared his throat again.

‘You can open your eyes now,’
he said.

Doing so, Farzana gleaned she was on a rooftop in the middle of a sprawling city. A city with a difference.

For it was floating in the middle of an ocean, billowing white clouds above. 'This is the first stop on the trail to your destiny,' the jinn explained.

'What is this place?' was all
Farzana could manage.
'Such questions are unimportant.'
'Then what is important?'

‘Backgammon,’
the mongoose expressed firmly.
‘*Backgammon*?’
‘How well do you play?’

The daughter of the forester
thought for a moment.
'Terribly.'

The mongoose beckoned the girl to lean down to his height. When she had done so, he touched a paw to her forehead and uttered an incantation, a spell of the rogue jinns.

'You are now the very finest backgammon player who's ever lived,' he said.

'How can I be?' Farzana crowed. 'I've only ever played twice, and I lost both times.'

The jinn widened his eyes.

'Think of backgammon,' he replied, 'and tell me what goes through your mind.' Farzana did as she had been asked, and found she could imagine the most complex winning strategies.

'That's astonishing,' she said. 'But...'

'But what?'

'But unless I am mistaken, a lot of backgammon is down to luck... luck of the dice.'

The mongoose smiled from
the corner of his mouth.
'That's where I can help,' he said.

The daughter of the forester took her place at a magnificent wooden board, the champion of the Floating Kingdom seated at the other side.

A weaselly little man with great tufts of hair sprouting from each ear, he regarded the stranger and laughed.

'You don't stand a chance against me,' he snapped haughtily. 'You're wasting my time!'

An hour later, the champion had been thrashed conclusively, the dice having not been in his favour. Farzana, on the other hand, had rolled double sixes time and again.

News of the trouncing spread through the Floating Kingdom like wildfire, then rippled across the ocean, and beyond.

During the bout of backgammon, the mongoose was nowhere to be seen. But as soon as Farzana had secured her place as champion, he reappeared.

'I won! I won!' she yelled jubilantly.
'You should have seen it! I got an amazing
run of double sixes!'
'Of course you did,' answered the
mongoose. 'For the little dice were
moving under jinn power.'

The next day, Farzana played a tournament in a city atop a mountain. Wrapped in furs, and confused as to where the jinn had transported her, she trounced her opponent again.

The day after that, she won a tournament in a sunken castle in an air pocket beneath a vast lake.

And after that, she won a fourth time,
at a caravanserai in the middle of the
Bleak Grim Desert.

By this time, word of Farzana's success had spread across the known world and had gained her the epithet 'Double Six'. But her skill, which was equalled by her luck, was not what people were talking about.

Rather, it was that she never
took her winnings.

Instead, she just left them, claiming that money was not what interested her. Whenever she pleaded with the mongoose to allow her to take a few of the gold coins, he would shake his head.

‘It’s not in your destiny,’ he would say.
‘Then what is my destiny?’ she would ask
in a forlorn voice.

'You will see,' the jinn would say. 'Keep playing, and keep winning, and you will reach your destiny soon enough.'

Now, it just so happened that Genghis Khan had a love for backgammon greater than anyone else alive, and he prided himself on his skill – derived from the fact that he, too, played with loaded dice.

It wasn't long before an invitation reached Farzana, borne across oceans and seas by a messenger from the imperial palace in Samarkand.

'Is this your doing?' she asked the mongoose.
'No, no, not at all,' came the reply. 'It's all
down to your skill.'
The jinn paused.

'Well, your skill, and a little luck
in the way of jinn-craft.'

The daughter of the forester held the invitation in her hands.

'Surely you know as well as I that Genghis Khan has a very bad reputation,' she said. 'He is famed for chopping the heads off people who cross him.'

The mongoose sighed.
'I could turn him into dust merely by blinking at him,' he said.
'That wouldn't be very kind,' replied Farzana.
'No less kind than he has been to half the known world.'

'So,' Farzana said, 'what should we do?'
'Accept the invitation, of course…
and enjoy the experience.'

In less time than it takes to tell, the jinn transported Farzana to the ancient capital of Samarkand, where the young backgammon champion was welcomed into the throne room with greater pomp and ceremony than any of the courtiers could remember.

A huge feast was prepared, along with all manner of entertainment.

Suddenly, as though tired of the festivities,
the emperor clapped his hands a single time.

Instantly, the acrobats melted away, as did the jugglers, the storytellers, and everyone else, as though fearful for their lives should they stay a moment longer.

The only people left in the throne room were Genghis Khan and Farzana, daughter of the forester and his wife.

‘Now we are alone,’ the emperor mused, ‘pray tell how you gained such skill in the game I so adore?’

Farzana strained to remain calm.
'A little bit of skill and a little bit of luck,
I suppose,' she said.

Genghis Khan slipped his guest a sideways glance. Smiling, he leaned towards her. ‘I hear that you play with a special pair of dice,’ he said.

'I have a pair, but am not sure
how special they are.'
'May I see them?' he asked.

Farzana fumbled in her pocket,
removed the dice, and passed them over.
Genghis Khan shook them between his hands,
then tossed them onto the low table
beside the divan.

A pair of threes.

Genghis Khan cocked his head in
the direction of the dice.
'Now *you* throw them,' he said.

Farzana did.

One, five.

The emperor frowned. Perhaps the dice were less loaded than his spies had led him to believe.

‘Shall we play a game?’ he asked.
‘I would be happy to,’
replied Farzana.

Genghis Khan clapped his hands.

A magnificent jewel-encrusted backgammon board was ushered in and set up on the low table.

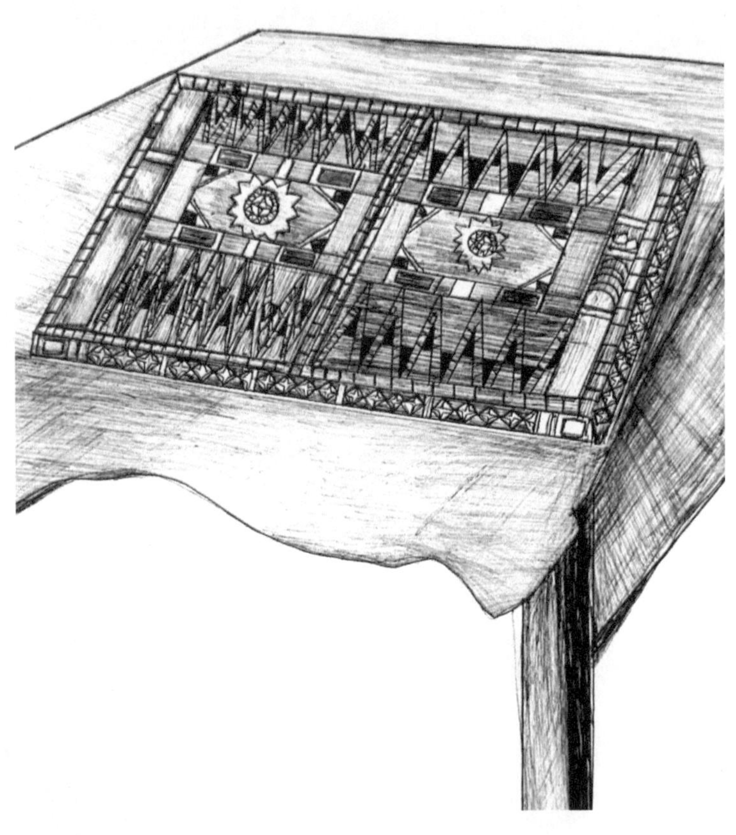

‘As the winner may not trust the loser,’ the emperor said, ‘I suggest that we play with neither your nor my dice.’

'Then, Your Majesty,' said Farzana, 'whose dice shall we play with?'

The khan clapped his hands again. 'Fresh dice will arrive in a moment or two,' he said.

As the emperor reclined on the divan, one of his equerries sped on horseback through the palace gates, down to the central square of Samarkand, snatched a pair of dice from the first backgammon board he saw, and hurried back to the palace with it.

Having been wiped with a silken cloth,
the dice were borne into the throne
room on a silk cushion.

Within a minute, the game had begun.

The jinn transferred himself from Farzana's dice to the pair that had just arrived. And, as is so easy to imagine in the realm of magical forces, he gave the emperor far less in the way of luck than he did the visitor.

Three games were played,
and Genghis Khan lost three times.

Enraged beyond words, he was about to have the visitor's head separated from her shoulders when something occurred to him.

Perhaps the girl had a jinn working for her, and it was that supernatural creature that had enabled her to win.

‘If I were to ask you very kindly to fill the far end of my throne room over there with rubies the size of pomegranates, could it be done?’

Farzana wished for the jinn to cast the spell
and, instantly, the rubies appeared.

The khan's eyes widened as they
had never widened before.
He held up a finger as though
testing the direction of the wind.

But Farzana shook her head.
‘No more conversation,’ she whispered.

A flash of blinding light came and went.

When the emperor's sight had returned,
he realized the visitor had vanished,
along with the glorious ruby treasure.

On the divan where Double Six had been seated was a simple wooden box. Curious as to what might be inside, Genghis Khan opened it, and found a scroll.

Unfurling it between outstretched hands,
he found a story…

The Tale of Double Six.

Holding it to the light, he began to read:

Once upon a time, when the clouds were pinker than pink and the great mountains were little higher than molehills, there lived a young woman named Farzana…

After adventures and triumphs worthy of the most fantastical realm, the emperor reached the final lines of the tale:

On the divan where Double Six had been seated was a simple wooden box. Curious as to what might be inside, Genghis Khan opened it, andfound a scroll. Unfurling it between outstretched hands, he found a story…

The Tale of Double Six.

Reaching the end, he had no way of knowing that the visitor had been transported back to her life deep in the forest – a life with a mother and a father who loved her very greatly indeed. Or that the fortune she so desired was not to beone measured in precious gems or gold coins.

The visitor may have vanished, along with
the rubies, but the tale remained.
A tale more precious than any treasure.

A tale so profound in its wisdom that the emperor had it inscribed into a piece of the finest marble and displayed in the great square of Samarkand – so that everyone could take advantage of its wisdom.

And there, hidden by the broken buildings of a fallen empire, it remains to this day, waiting for the adventurer who shall find it.

But that is another story.

Finis

About the Author

Descended from a long line of storytellers, writers, and savants, Tahir Shah is one of the most prolific authors of his generation. He has published more than sixty books in numerous genres, including travel, fiction, and fantasy, as well as tales for children.

Raised in the tradition of Eastern 'teaching stories', Shah is passionate about stories and storytelling. He regards the ability to learn from folklore as being in us all, what he calls a 'default setting of humankind'. As well as having written scores of books, Shah has made documentaries for National Geographic TV and The History Channel. He is the founder and CEO of the charity, The Scheherazade Foundation.

About the Artist

Misbah Bukhari grew up as the youngest in her family in Pakistan. She gained a fine arts degree from university in Islamabad and since then has developed her skills across a variety of mediums, though she prefers to get her hands dirty with paints and charcoals. Misbah enjoys weaving reality with the imaginary, and aims to express her own spirit and individuality through the characters she draws.

Books By Tahir Shah

Travel

Trail of Feathers
Travels With Myself
Beyond the Devil's Teeth
In Search of King Solomon's Mines
House of the Tiger King
In Arabian Nights
The Caliph's House
Sorcerer's Apprentice
Journey Through Namibia

Novels

Jinn Hunter: Book One – The Prism
Jinn Hunter: Book Two – The Jinnslayer
Jinn Hunter: Book Three – The Perplexity
Hannibal Fogg and the Supreme Secret of Man
Hannibal Fogg and the Codex Cartographica
Casablanca Blues
Eye Spy
Godman
Paris Syndrome
Timbuctoo

Nasrudin

Travels With Nasrudin
The Misadventures of the Mystifying Nasrudin
The Peregrinations of the Perplexing Nasrudin
The Voyages and Vicissitudes of Nasrudin
Nasrudin in the Land of Fools

Teaching Stories

The Arabian Nights Adventures
Scorpion Soup
Tales Told to a Melon
The Afghan Notebook
The Caravanserai Stories
Ghoul Brothers
Hourglass
Imaginist
Jinn's Treasure
Jinnlore
Mellified Man
Skeleton Island
Wellspring
When the Sun Forgot to Rise
Outrunning the Reaper
The Cap of Invisibility
On Backgammon Time
The Wondrous Seed
The Paradise Tree
Mouse House
The Hoopoe's Flight
The Old Wind
A Treasury of Tales
Daydreams of an Octopus & Other Stories

Miscellaneous

The Reason to Write
Zigzag Think
Being Myself

Research

Cultural Research

The Middle East Bedside Book

Three Essays

Anthologies

The Anthologies

The Clockmaker's Box

The Tahir Shah Fiction Reader

The Tahir Shah Travel Reader

Edited by

Congress With a Crocodile

A Son of a Son, Volume I

A Son of a Son, Volume II

Screenplays

Casablanca Blues: The Screenplay

Timbuctoo: The Screenplay

A REQUEST

If you enjoyed this book, please review it on your favourite online retailer or review website.

Reviews are an author's best friend.

To stay in touch with Tahir Shah, and to hear about his upcoming releases before anyone else, please sign up for his mailing list:

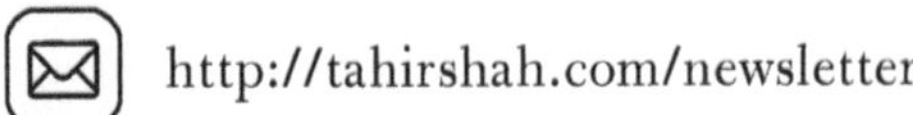
http://tahirshah.com/newsletter

And to follow him on social media, please go to any of the following links:

http://www.twitter.com/humanstew

@tahirshah999

http://www.facebook.com/TahirShahAuthor

http://www.youtube.com/user/tahirshah999

http://www.pinterest.com/tahirshah

https://www.goodreads.com/tahirshahauthor

http://www.tahirshah.com

www.ingramcontent.com/pod-product-compliance
Lightning Source LLC
Chambersburg PA
CBHW030521310726
48979CB00010B/1756/J

* 9 7 8 1 9 1 4 9 6 0 9 8 7 *